DATE DUE

DEC 0 1 2012		
APR 0 1 2013		
APR 1 5 2013		
APR 2 5 2014		
OCT 0 1 2014		
GAYLORD		PRINTED IN U.S.A.

THE SLEEPING BEAUTY

RETOLD AND ILLUSTRATED BY
WARWICK HUTTON

A MARGARET K. MC ELDERRY BOOK

ATHENEUM   1979   NEW YORK

for Lizzie

Library of Congress Cataloging in Publication Data
Grimm, Jacob Ludwig Karl, 1785-1863.
The sleeping beauty.
"A Margaret K. McElderry book."
SUMMARY: Enraged at not being invited to the
princess' christening, the wicked fairy casts a spell
that dooms the princess to sleep for 100 years.
[1. Fairy tales. 2. Folklore—Germany] I. Grimm,
Wilhelm Karl, 1786-1859, joint author. II. Hutton,
Warwick. III. Title.
PZ8.G882S 1979   389.2'1'0943   78-64772
ISBN 0-689-50131-5

A long time ago there lived a King and Queen. Every day they said sadly, "Oh, if only we had a child," but they never had one.

It happened one day, when the Queen was bathing, that a frog climbed out of the water and said to her, "Your wish shall at last come true. Before a year has passed, you shall have a daughter."

It came about exactly as the frog had said. The Queen had a little girl, and she was so beautiful that the King was overcome with delight and ordered a huge feast to be prepared. He invited not only his relations and friends, but also the Wise Women of the kingdom, so they would bless the child. There were thirteen Wise Women, but unfortunately only twelve golden plates could be found in the royal kitchens, so one of the thirteen was not invited.

The feast was celebrated with great splendor, and the Wise Women presented the child with their magic gifts. One of them gave virtue, another beauty, a third wealth, and soon the Princess had been given everything one could wish for in this world.

When eleven of the Wise Women had given their presents, quite suddenly the thirteenth appeared at the door. Furious at not having been invited, and without greeting anybody, or even looking at them, she screamed in revenge, "The King's daughter shall prick herself on a spindle in her fifteenth year and fall down dead!" Without uttering another word she turned and left the hall.

Everybody looked at each other in shock and horror. Then the twelfth Wise Woman, who had not yet made her wish, came forward. Although she could not undo the bad spell, she did her best to soften it by saying, "It shall not be death into which the Princess shall fall, but a deep sleep of a hundred years."

The King, who wanted desperately to protect the child he loved so much from this calamity, gave orders that every spindle and spinning wheel in the whole kingdom should be burned at once.

As the young girl grew up, all the gifts of the Wise Women fulfilled themselves. She was beautiful, good, friendly, and sensible. Everybody who met her loved and cherished her.

By chance it happened that on the day she was fifteen years old, the Princess was left alone in the castle, for both the King and Queen were away traveling in their kingdom. She explored everywhere, looking into halls and chambers, and before long she wandered into an unknown part of the castle. She came, at length, to an old tower with narrow winding stairs leading up, and she climbed carefully until she reached a little door.

The lock on the door had a rusty key, and when she turned it the door sprang open. There, in a little room, sat an old woman with a spindle, busily spinning her flax.

"Good day, old mother," said the King's daughter. "What are you doing there?"

"I spin," said the woman and nodded her head.

"What is that little thing that jumps about so gaily?" said the Princess; and quickly she moved forward and took the spindle to try and spin too. Hardly had she touched it than the spell began to work. She pricked her finger and it bled.

She sank down onto the bed that stood there and fell into a deep sleep.

This sleep spread over the whole castle. The King and Queen, who had just arrived back, began to feel sleep overpowering them as they stepped into the hall, and soon the whole court lay down and slept with them.

The horses in the stables slept. The dogs in the yard, the pigeons on the roof, and even the flies on the wall slept. In the royal kitchens, as the fire that flickered in the range grew still, the joint stopped roasting, and the cook, who was just about to hit the scullery boy for his rudeness, stopped and fell asleep as he stood.

The wind died down, and in the trees by the castle not a single leaf moved.

Around the castle a hedge of thorns began to grow, which reached higher every year and at last covered the whole castle and grew above it, so that nothing of the castle could be seen, not even the flag.

A tale about the beautiful, sleeping "Briar Rose," for that was the name of the King's daughter, began to be told, and it soon spread throughout the kingdom. From time to time Princes came who wanted to break through the hedge, to get to the castle. But it always proved impossible; the thorns clung together like hands. Indeed, some young men got caught, for the thorns closed upon anyone who tried to penetrate them. In time, the forest's secret was forgotten.

After many years another Prince came into the kingdom, and he overheard an old man talking about the hedge of thorns. He listened fascinated to the tale of an overgrown castle that was supposed to be there, of the beautiful Princess called Briar Rose, who had been sleeping for a hundred years, and of how around her the King and Queen and the whole court slept too.

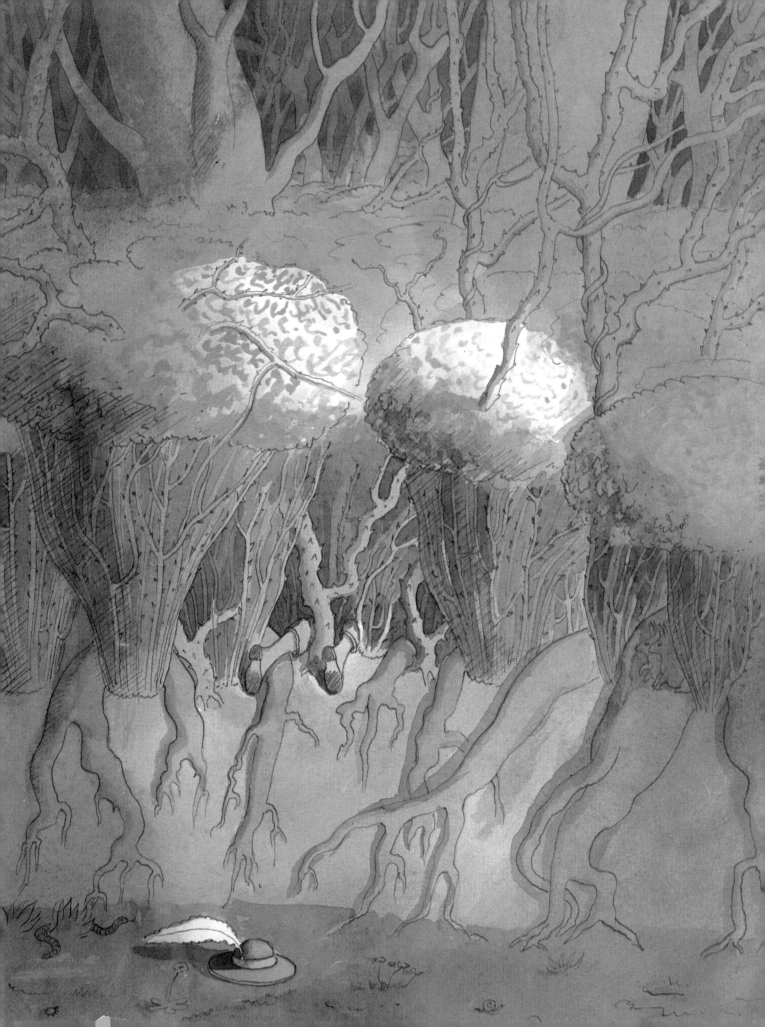

The old man told how his grandfather could remember many young men trying to penetrate the thorns, but that all had failed, and some had even stuck fast in the attempt.

The Prince said, "I'm not afraid. I must get through and see the beautiful Briar Rose."

The good old man tried again and again to dissuade him, but the Prince would not listen to any warning.

By chance, exactly one hundred years had passed, and it was now the time for Briar Rose to wake up. When the Prince approached the hedge of thorns, they seemed to blossom and part by themselves to let him through unharmed. Behind him the thorns closed again.

He reached the castle and peered around the entrance. There he saw an extraordinary sight. In the bright daylight, guards and speckled hounds were both lying asleep. When he looked up, pigeons on the roof had their heads under their wings.

He went on and entered the living quarters. The flies on the wall slept. The cook slept standing up, with his hand ready to strike the scullery boy, who also slept. Behind them sat a servant woman deep in sleep with a chicken in her lap half plucked.

The Prince went farther, and in the big hall he found the whole court lying asleep, with the King and Queen sleeping on their thrones. He went farther still, and everything was so hushed and quiet that he could even hear the sound of his own breathing.

At last he came to the tower and climbed the stairs and opened the door of the little room in which Briar Rose was sleeping. There she lay. She looked so beautiful that the Prince could not take his eyes off her. He bent down and gave her a kiss.

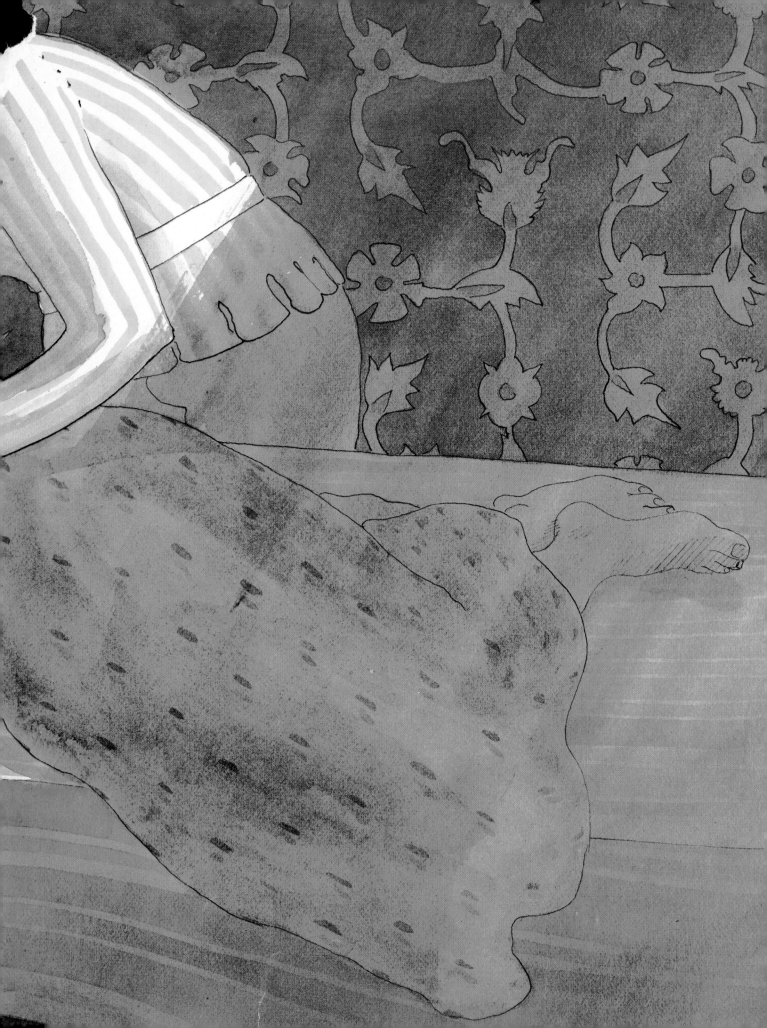

As the kiss touched her, Briar Rose opened her eyes, looked up, and smiled at the Prince. Together they came down to the great hall as the King and Queen woke up, and then the whole court rubbed their eyes and looked at each other in astonishment.

Outside in the courtyard, the guards awoke; the hounds jumped up, shook themselves, and wagged their tails; the pigeons on the rooftops took their heads from under their wings, looked about, and flew off into the distant fields.

The flies began to creep about on the wall again; the fire rose up, crackled, and started to cook the food. The joint began to sizzle, and the cook gave the scullery boy such a smack that he cried, while behind them the servant woman went on plucking the chicken.

Then the wedding of the Prince and Briar Rose was celebrated with great rejoicing, and they both lived happily to the end of their days.